P9-CQV-688

DISCARD

Bloomington Public Library

JAN   2018

NISSAND

Wendy Saves the Day!

Adapted by Elizabeth Milton
Based on the episode "Saffi's Tree House" written by Miranda Larson

LITTLE, BROWN & COMPANY
LB kids

© 2016 HIT Entertainment Limited and Keith Chapman. The Bob the Builder name and character, related characters and logo are trademarks of HIT Entertainment Limited.

© 2016 HIT Entertainment Limited.
All rights reserved.

All rights reserved. In accordance with the U.S. Copyright Act of 1976, the scanning, uploading, and electronic sharing of any part of this book without the permission of the publisher is unlawful piracy and theft of the author's intellectual property. If you would like to use material from the book (other than for review purposes), prior written permission must be obtained by contacting the publisher at permissions@hbgusa.com. Thank you for your support of the author's rights.

Little, Brown and Company

Hachette Book Group
1290 Avenue of the Americas, New York, NY 10104
Visit us at lb-kids.com
bobthebuilder.com

LB kids is an imprint of Little, Brown and Company.
The LB kids name and logo are trademarks of Hachette Book Group, Inc.

The publisher is not responsible for websites (or their content) that are not owned by the publisher.

First Edition: October 2016

Library of Congress Control Number: 2016933885

ISBN 978-0-316-27294-0

10 9 8 7 6 5 4 3 2 1

CW

Printed in the United States of America

It was a beautiful day in Spring City. Bob, Wendy, and the team were gathered around a giant tree in Saffi's backyard, ready to begin a special project: a tree house!

"I want it to be the Spring City Rockets' first clubhouse!" Saffi told JJ, Mila, and Brandon.

Saffi had made a drawing of a tree house with a sloped roof, a viewing deck, a zip line, a rope ladder, and a flag. It looked wonderful—but very difficult to build!

Bob was surprised when he saw the complicated drawing. "It's not quite what we had planned..." he told Saffi.

"Wendy's my hero, and she can build anything. Right, Wendy?" Saffi said. "And we can have our first meeting in the new clubhouse today at dinnertime?"

"Your hero, eh?" Wendy smiled. "How can I say no to that?"

"Okay, team!" Bob said. "We're building a fancy tree house in just one day. It's your job, hero Wendy, so I think you'd better say it this time."

"Really, Bob? Okay, then!" Wendy cleared her throat. "Can we build it?"

"YES, WE CAN!" Bob and the team called out.

Wendy looked at her clipboard. "We're going to need a new schedule!" she said. She asked Bob and Muck to go back to Bob's Yard to cut timber for the support beams.

"Lofty, you can stay here and help me," she added, "and I'll call Dizzy to pour cement for the foundations!"

The build had begun!

Bob headed to the Yard and began to measure the beams.
He didn't hear Scoop arrive.

"What are you doing Bob?" Scoop asked.

Bob was so startled, he let go of his measuring tape! *"Ow!"*
he yelped, as it rolled up and hit his fingers. "Scoop, I'm cutting
these beams! If you're bored, could you straighten up rocks from
the delivery?" Scoop agreed, and Bob got back to work.

Meanwhile, in Saffi's backyard, Wendy mixed together blue and red paint. Then she applied the new purple paint onto the floor panel for the tree house's deck.

Wendy happily checked the tasks off her list. "Floor painted. Check! Paint drying. Check!"

Just then, Saffi stopped by with furniture and decorations.
"I'm here to get the tree house ready!"

But Wendy didn't hear Saffi...or notice her arranging a rug
and chairs on the freshly painted floor panel.

"Saffi, wait! The paint's not dry!" Wendy yelled, but it was too late. Wendy pulled up an edge of the rug from on top of the floor panel. Sure enough, the wet paint had smeared!

"There's been a change to the schedule," Wendy called over to Lofty. "Instead of hanging the rope ladder, I'm repainting the floor!"

When she was done, Wendy called Bob at the Yard to check in. "I still have to hang the zip line," she told him. "As soon as Muck arrives with the support beams, I'll have Dizzy pour the cement."

"Muck is on the way," Bob said, "but what about the flag?"

"There's a flag? I don't have that on the schedule!" Wendy said, panicked.

"Don't worry, Wendy, I'll make one"—Bob paused—"*after*
I fix my workbench!"

Bob had just seen Scoop, who was moving rocks from the
delivery, back up too quickly and knock over the workbench!

Back at the site, Wendy hung the zip line, Muck dropped off the support beams, and Dizzy began to pour cement. "Okay, everything's ready," Wendy said. "We just need Bob to bring the flag!"

That's when Saffi came by again. "I had the best idea! We can put our trophy inside the tree house!" she told Wendy.

"Saffi, wait," Wendy warned her. "The cement has to dry for the tree house to be strong and sturdy."

"I can wait!" said Saffi.

Bob had the flag and was ready to go, when he saw that Scoop had organized the rocks...in a very unique way!

"It might work better if you stack the *largest* rocks on the ground," Bob told Scoop. "But let's try that later. First, we have a flag to deliver!"

They went to Saffi's backyard...

...and arrived to find Saffi in danger! She was standing on the deck of the tree house, but hadn't waited for the cement to dry, so the deck was wobbling.

"Oh no! Saffi!" said Bob.

Suddenly, there was a loud creak as the support beams slipped out of place.

"Help!" Saffi yelled as she—and the deck—began to fall!

Saffi slid off the deck...but luckily Bob was there to catch her!
When they were a safe distance away, he asked, "Why were you up there, Saffi?"

Saffi's lip quivered. "I thought I had waited long enough for the cement to dry, but I guess I was wrong!" There was another loud creak, and the deck tilted even more. Saffi gasped. "Our trophy! It's still up there!"

"Don't worry, Saffi, I'll get it!" Wendy said, still wearing her safety harness.

Wendy climbed the tree and tried to reach the trophy, but it was too far away. Bob grabbed the harness line and lowered Wendy until she was dangling just above the trophy, and Wendy grabbed it!

"Okay, Bob! Get me out of here!" Wendy yelled.

Bob pulled on the harness line, hoisting up Wendy above the deck. She grabbed the zip line with one hand and held the trophy in the other.

As the deck broke apart, Wendy used the zip line to reach the ground.

Saffi ran up to Wendy. "My hero!" she said, and gave Wendy a big hug.

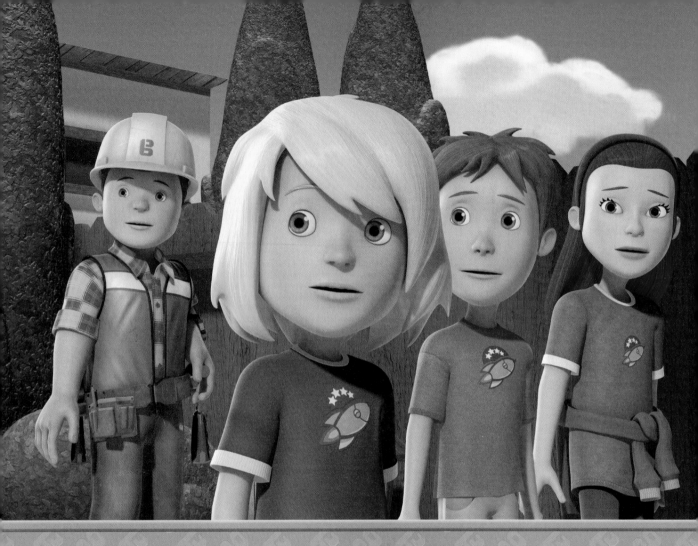

Just then, the rest of the Spring City Rockets came by to
see how the clubhouse was coming along.

"What happened?" JJ asked when he saw the broken deck.

"I'm so sorry," Saffi told her friends. "I didn't wait for the
cement to dry, and now we don't have a clubhouse!"

"We've still got time to fix it. Right, Wendy?" Bob asked.

Wendy nodded, and walked over to Muck, Lofty, and Scoop. "Team, there's a new schedule, and I need all wheels on deck!"

The Spring City Rockets painted a new flag. Bob straightened the support beams as Dizzy poured new cement around them. Muck lifted up wood panels that Wendy used to fix the deck. Then Lofty carefully lowered the tree house onto it.

Finally, Wendy put the flag on the roof, and the Spring City Rockets' first clubhouse was complete!

Saffi watched patiently as Bob and Wendy checked the support beams.

Brandon, JJ, and Mila came running over, excited to see the finished tree house!

"Hold on!" Saffi told them. "We have to make sure the cement is dry. Right, hero Wendy?"

"Right, Saffi!" Wendy smiled.

Bob tested the cement, and it was dry! Everyone cheered!

Saffi, Brandon, JJ, and Mila climbed the rope ladder and explored the clubhouse.

"So, what do you think?" Bob called up to them.

"I want one!" they all yelled.

Bob laughed. "Have room in your schedule for three more tree houses, Wendy?"

"Of course!" Wendy said, without missing a beat. "I am a *hero* after all!"